THE PRINCE OF EGYPT

BROTHERS IN EGYPT

ADAPTED BY DAVID A. ADLER

DREAMWORKS™

PUFFIN BOOKS
Published by the Penguin Group
Penguin Putnam Books for Young Readers,
345 Hudson Street, New York, New York 10014, U.S.A.
Penguin Books Ltd, 27 Wrights Lane, London W8 5TZ, England
Penguin Books Australia Ltd, Ringwood, Victoria, Australia
Penguin Books Canada Ltd, 10 Alcorn Avenue, Toronto, Ontario, Canada M4V 3B2
Penguin Books (N.Z.) Ltd, 182-190 Wairau Road, Auckland 10, New Zealand

Penguin Books Ltd, Registered Offices: Harmondsworth, Middlesex, England

Published by Puffin Books, a member of Penguin Putnam Books for Young Readers, 1998

1 3 5 7 9 10 8 6 4 2

TM & © 1998 DreamWorks

Printed in the United States of America

This book is based on the film *The Prince of Egypt* and not the Bible.
The Biblical account of this story can be found in the book of Exodus.

TABLE of CONTENTS

PROLOGUE: A MOTHER'S FAREWELL   5

CHAPTER ONE: THE RACE   9

CHAPTER TWO: SETI'S REPRIMAND   15

CHAPTER THREE: BROTHERLY LOVE   19

CHAPTER FOUR: THE BANQUET   25

CHAPTER FIVE: THE SHOCKING TRUTH   31

CHAPTER SIX: A NIGHTMARE   37

CHAPTER SEVEN: RAMESES' PLANS   41

CHAPTER EIGHT: A NEW LIFE   47

CHAPTER NINE: A DESERT MIRACLE   51

CHAPTER TEN: BITTERSWEET REUNION   57

EPILOGUE: JOURNEY TO FREEDOM   61

PROLOGUE
A MOTHER'S FAREWELL

It was hot in Goshen, a village in the eastern section of Egypt. The Hebrew slaves lived there, and when they were not working, building the temples, monuments, and palaces of Egypt, they stayed in the cool shade of their homes. But today, the women were not hiding from the heat. They were hiding from Egyptian soldiers who stormed through the village. The guards were searching for babies, to carry out Pharaoh's decree that all newborn Hebrew boys be drowned.

In one home, Yocheved huddled in a corner, holding her infant son. Her older children, Miriam and Aaron, crouched nearby.

Miriam peered through the window. In the alley outside, she could see the Egyptian soldiers. She watched one soldier push a mother and her baby to the ground. Another soldier grabbed the baby from her arms.

Miriam turned from the window.

"We have to hurry," she warned her mother. "There are soldiers outside."

Yocheved looked at her baby boy. She wiped a tear from her cheek and cradled him in her arms.

"Take the basket," she whispered to Miriam.

Yocheved looked out the window and waited. When the alley was clear, she ran outside with the baby in her arms. Miriam and Aaron followed her.

They moved quickly and quietly in the shadows. Finally, they came to the bank of the Nile River. There, at the edge of the water, Yocheved looked at her baby and said, "My good, sweet son, don't be afraid, do not fear."

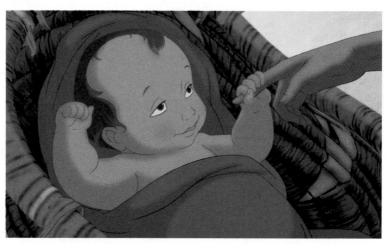

She paused, wiped a tear from her eye, and whispered, "My son, I have nothing I can give, but this chance that you may live. I pray we'll meet again."

Yocheved gently placed her baby in the basket. Before she closed the lid, she looked at him for one last time and began to sing,

Hush now, my baby,
Be still, love, don't cry.
Sleep as you're rocked by the stream.
Sleep and remember
My last lullaby
So I'll be with you when you dream. . . .

Yocheved placed the basket in the water and watched tearfully as the river carried it off.

At first the basket floated slowly in the water. Then, as the current picked up, the basket spun around and moved quickly. It swept past a surprised hippopotamus and the open mouth of a hungry crocodile.

Miriam was frightened for her brother. She ran along the bank of the river to see what would happen to him.

She watched in horror as a huge barge, powered by dozens of rowers, headed straight at the basket. Then, just before the barge crashed into it, an oar pushed it out of the way. From there, the basket floated into a placid pool near Pharaoh's palace.

Miriam hid in the reeds. She saw the Queen of Egypt standing there in the water. Her young son, Rameses, was with her.

Miriam watched the Queen draw the basket up from the water. She held her breath as she saw the Queen open it and look at the baby. She remembered what her mother had told the baby, *"Don't be afraid, do not fear."*

The Queen lifted the baby from the basket, touched his cheek, and smiled. Miriam saw how gentle the Queen was with her brother and knew he would be safe.

"Brother," Miriam whispered, "you're safe now, and safe may you stay. For I have a prayer just for you: Grow, baby brother. Come back some day. Come and deliver us, too."

The Queen named the baby "Moses," which means "I drew him out." She drew him out of the water and turned to her young son. "Come, Rameses," she said to him. "We will show Pharaoh your new baby brother, Moses."

Miriam watched as the Queen brought Moses to the palace. He would be raised as her son, a prince of Egypt. And he would have a new brother, Rameses.

CHAPTER ONE
THE RACE

The Hebrew people were slaves of Pharaoh. They were forced to cut straw and make it into bricks, and to haul large stones. It was not an easy life.

But Moses had a privileged childhood. He grew up as a prince in Pharaoh's palace. He was the brother of Rameses, the heir to the throne.

When Moses and Rameses were young children, they played together as brothers and best friends. They continued to play together when they were older.

One day, Moses and Rameses raced horse-drawn chariots through the streets near the palace. "Faster," Rameses shouted to his horses. He urged them on with the reins. "Faster! Faster! You run like mules!"

Moses pulled his chariot up alongside Rameses. He pretended it took no effort to catch up to his older brother.

Moses called to Rameses. "How would you like to have your face on a stone wall?"

"Yes," Rameses shouted over the noise of the chariots.

"One day I will," he added.

"How about now?" Moses asked.

Moses swerved his chariot and banged into Rameses. He forced Rameses into the stone wall along the side of the road. Moses laughed and rode quickly ahead.

"Hey," Rameses cried. "You almost killed me!" Moses laughed. "I was only having fun," he explained.

"Oh, so it's fun you want," Rameses said. "I'll give you fun!"

With that, Rameses sped off. He raced up a ramp and onto the top of a great stone wall. Moses charged along the road below.

"Admit it, Moses," he called down to his brother. "You've always looked up to me."

"Yes, but it's not much of a view!" Moses joked.

When Rameses rode down the ramp on the other end of the stone wall, Moses caught up with him. The race continued.

Soon, Moses and Rameses came to a marketplace. Vendors were selling pottery, cloth, spices, fruits, and vegetables. People were talking and shopping. Two men were playing the ancient Egyptian version of chess.

Moses and Rameses charged through the area. They hardly noticed the havoc they caused as they sped by, sending people and their wares flying through the air.

They raced on into the temple courtyard. Hotep and Huy, the Egyptian high priests, were there performing a ritual. Hundreds of slaves were working there, too. They were building a great monument to the boys' father, the Pharaoh Seti.

As the boys rode by, they knocked into a ladder which supported a large scaffold. On top of the scaffold was a slave carrying a heavy load of bricks. The slave fell. The load of bricks banged against the immense bust of Seti, knocking off the nose. But Moses and Rameses barely noticed.

They continued on, driving their chariots to the top of a huge mound of sand. They rested there for a moment and laughed happily from the excitement of their race.

Suddenly, the wall that held back the mound of sand began to creak under them. Then it gave way, and sent Moses and Rameses surfing down an enormous wave of sand.

Down below, Huy turned and saw the wave coming toward him. He tried to warn Hotep. But before he could say anything, the sand swept over them. The priests were buried.

The boys stopped to watch as the priests dug themselves out. As they looked at the damage they had caused, Rameses grew concerned. "Do you think we'll get in trouble?" he asked Moses.

Moses was used to his brother's worrying. As heir to the throne, he was often anxious about what Seti might think. But Moses was sure there would be no trouble this time. He smiled and reassured his brother.

"No, not a chance," he told Rameses.

But Moses was wrong. He and Rameses *did* get in trouble.

CHAPTER TWO
SETI'S REPRIMAND

Later that afternoon, Rameses and Moses were brought before their father, the Pharaoh. He glared down at the boys from his throne.

"Why do the gods torment me with such reckless, destructive, blasphemous sons?" he asked angrily.

"Father, please," Rameses began. "Let me explain."

"Be still!" Seti snapped. "Pharaoh speaks!"

He stared at Rameses. "I seek to build an empire, and your only thought is to amuse yourselves by tearing it down," he scolded.

Rameses and Moses looked down, too ashamed to face their father.

"Have I taught you nothing?" Pharaoh asked.

At that moment, the two priests stepped forward.

"Oh, Your Majesty, you're an excellent teacher," Hotep assured Pharaoh.

"Oh, yes," Huy added. "It's not your fault that your sons learned nothing."

"Well," said Hotep quickly, hoping to have the last

word. "They did learn blasphemy."

"Enough!" Pharaoh declared, casting a hard look at Hotep and Huy. They bowed and hurried from the room.

When the priests were gone, Moses looked up at Pharaoh. "Father," he said, "I goaded Rameses on. I am responsible."

"*Responsible!*" Seti exclaimed. He turned to Rameses and asked, "Do you know the meaning of that word?"

"Yes, father, I understand," Rameses said softly.

"And do you understand the task for which your birth has destined you?" Seti continued.

Rameses, his head down, nodded.

Moses stood quietly next to Rameses. He tried to catch his brother's eye, to offer him some support. But Rameses did not look up.

"Do you know our ancient traditions?" Seti continued. "When I pass into the Next World, you will be Pharaoh. You will be the morning and the evening star," he reminded his oldest son.

Rameses began to protest. "One damaged temple does not destroy centuries of tradition," he told his father.

"But one weak link can break the chain of a mighty dynasty!" Seti thundered, furious.

The Queen stepped forward and gently placed her hand on Seti's arm, to calm him.

Seti looked at his wife, then back at his son.

"I've said enough," he told Rameses, no longer shouting. "You have my leave to go."

"But father," Rameses began.

The Queen looked at Rameses. With a slight shake of her head she signaled him to be silent.

Rameses understood. He bowed to his father and left the room.

When Rameses was gone, Moses spoke up again.

"Father, you know it was really all my fault," Moses said. "You should have yelled at me, not Rameses."

"Moses," Seti said. "You will never have his burdens. One day I will pass my crown to Rameses. He must not let himself be led astray. Not even by you, my son."

Moses knew that Seti was only trying to prepare his

brother for the responsibility he would carry later in life. Still, he felt bad that their race had gotten Rameses in so much trouble. There had to be something he could say to make the situation better.

"All Rameses cares about is your approval," Moses said. "I know he will live up to your expectations. He only needs the opportunity."

Seti looked down at his younger son. He nodded his head slowly and said, "Maybe so." Seti paused for a moment, then said, "Go now. I will see you both tonight at the banquet."

CHAPTER THREE
BROTHERLY LOVE

Moses left Pharaoh and went to a small room at the side of the palace where he knew he would find his brother. Rameses always went to that room when he was upset. And Moses always followed him there to cheer him up.

Moses didn't see Rameses, but he was sure he was there. He leaned against the base of a large statue and began speaking. "Well," he said, trying to sound upbeat. "That went well."

"Just go away," said an unhappy voice.

Moses looked up. His brother was sitting in the lap of the stone statue.

"The weak link in the chain," Rameses said unhappily. "That's what he called me!"

"Well, you are rather pathetic," Moses teased, trying to raise his brother's spirits.

"Irresponsible! Ignorant of the traditions!" Rameses went on. "He practically accused me of bringing down the dynasty."

Moses heard the hurt in his brother's voice. He tried to cheer him.

"Yes," Moses joked. "I can see it now. Because of you, the pyramids will collapse and the mighty sphinx will crumble."

Moses continued to tease his brother as he walked over to a table near the balcony. On the table was a large punch bowl.

"Because of you, the Nile River will dry up," Moses went on. "You alone will ruin Egypt, the greatest kingdom on earth."

While Moses talked, he poured punch from the bowl into a large bag. Then he held up the bag and dangled it over the edge of the balcony.

"This is all very funny to you, isn't it?" Rameses asked. He jumped down and landed in front of Moses. "Tell me something, Moses," Rameses demanded. "Why is it that every time *you* start something *I* get in trouble?"

Moses didn't answer. He just grinned and dropped the bag.

Rameses rushed to the edge of the balcony and leaned over. At the same time, Moses ducked down out of sight.

Down below, the water bag landed on Hotep and Huy. They looked up and saw Rameses.

"That's it!" Hotep yelled. "You're in trouble now!"

"Get down here!" Huy shouted. "You owe us an apology!"

Moses laughed. Then he lifted the bowl of punch off

the table and handed it to Rameses.

"You're already in big trouble," Moses pointed out. "You may as well have some fun."

Rameses shrugged and smiled. "You're right," he agreed. "I may as well." Rameses leaned over the edge of the balcony and dumped the contents of the bowl onto the two priests.

Hotep, now drenched, looked up and shook his fist. "By the eye of Ra, you'll pay for this!" he yelled.

"Your father will hear about this," Huy added.

Rameses smiled. He was no longer thinking about his father. He was just grateful to have a brother like Moses. Somehow, Moses always knew exactly what to do to make him smile. Moses draped his arms across his brother's shoulders and pulled him close.

"You know," Moses said to Rameses as they began walking toward the corridor. "I figured out what your problem is."

"What?" Rameses asked.

"It's not that you don't care," Moses told him. "It's that you care too much."

"And your problem, dear brother," Rameses told him, "is that you don't care enough."

"Oh," Moses said. "Then I suppose you care a lot more than I do that we're late for the banquet."

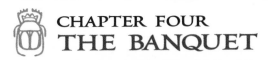

CHAPTER FOUR
THE BANQUET

Moses and Rameses ran through the palace halls. When they reached the doors of the banquet room, Rameses whispered, "I'm done for. Father will kill me."

"Don't worry," Moses told him. "No one will even notice that we're late."

Rameses took a deep breath, then slowly opened the huge doors.

The boys stepped inside and found themselves on a large stage. As soon as they entered, the crowd of dignitaries stood and clapped.

"No one will even notice!" Rameses muttered to Moses.

Before Moses could respond, the Queen came over to them. She hugged Rameses.

"They're cheering for you," she told him. "Your father has just named you Prince Regent. You are now responsible for overseeing the building of all the temples."

Rameses was surprised. Earlier, his father had yelled at him. He called him reckless and destructive. He had even called him a weak link! Now, he was entrusting him with a very important position.

Rameses looked at his mother.

She smiled. "I suggest you go thank your father," she told him.

As Ramses hurried over to Pharaoh, the Queen turned to Moses. "It seems that someone convinced your father that Rameses just needs the opportunity," she said with a smile.

Moses smiled back. Then he gazed over at his brother. Rameses would make a fine Prince Regent. Moses was sure of it.

Then Moses spotted Hotep and Huy. He remembered how they had gotten Moses and Rameses in trouble with Pharaoh.

It's time they showed Rameses some respect, he thought.

Stepping forward, he said, "I propose that the high priests offer some tribute to their new regent."

"That's an excellent idea," Seti agreed.

Hotep and Huy bowed to Seti. Then they leaned forward and whispered to each other.

Moses and Rameses stood together. They wondered what gift the priests would offer.

Huy hurried from the room as Hotep began a chant.

"By the power of Ra," he called out, "we present for your delight an exotic treasure stolen from a faraway land."

There was a sudden blast of smoke. When it settled, Moses and Rameses saw Huy standing next to a large object covered by a cloth.

Hotep pulled away the cloth to reveal a woman seated on a camel. Her hands were tied with a rope.

She was the most beautiful woman Moses had ever seen. He looked at his brother, and he could tell that Rameses admired her beauty, too.

"We offer you this delicate desert flower from the land of Midian," Hotep said.

Huy pulled on the rope, and the girl fell to the floor.

"Let us inspect this desert flower," Rameses said. He walked toward the girl, whose name was Tzipporah.

But as Rameses got close to Tzipporah, she snarled at him. Then she tried to bite him.

Rameses backed off. "She's more of a desert cobra," he declared.

"You're not much of a snake charmer, are you?" Moses teased his brother.

"That's why I give her to you," Rameses said. He pushed Moses toward Tzipporah, and put the rope in his hands.

"I don't belong to anyone," Tzipporah protested. "Especially not to a pampered palace brat."

Moses was shocked. How dare she speak to him this way?

He cast a glance at his brother, the newly appointed Prince Regent, then turned back to Tzipporah. "You must show the proper respect for a prince of Egypt," he told her.

"I am showing you the respect you deserve," she told him. "None!"

Moses held the rope tightly as Tzipporah struggled to pull away from him.

"Let me go!" she cried.

"As you wish," Moses said. He let go of the rope. When he did, Tzipporah lost her balance and fell back into the reflecting pool.

"Dry her off," Rameses commanded one of the royal guards. "Then take her to my brother's chambers."

After she had been carried away, Rameses turned to his father. "My first act as regent is to appoint my brother Moses Royal Chief Architect," he said.

Smiling, Rameses held out a ring and put it on Moses' finger.

Pharaoh nodded, acknowledging the close bond between his sons. Despite their recklessness, he was proud of them.

After the banquet, Moses returned to his chambers, expecting to find the beautiful Tzipporah waiting for him.

As he entered, he saw a figure on the bed, behind a curtain. Moses smiled. He pulled the curtain, and was surprised to find one of the palace guards. He was tied with the rope that had once bound Tzipporah.

Moses hurried to the window. He saw the sheets and curtains tied together and hanging down. He looked out the window and saw Tzipporah quietly leading her camel away from the palace.

CHAPTER FIVE
THE SHOCKING TRUTH

Moses hurried down to the courtyard. Two guards were on watch.

"Guards!" he called out, trying to distract them before they noticed Tzipporah.

The guards turned and bowed to him.

"There's a man in my room," he told them. "Please, look into it."

"Right away, Sire," they said, and rushed way.

When they were gone, Moses turned back to look for Tzipporah. But he was too late. She had gotten away. He ran after her, intrigued by her will and beauty. He followed as she made her way into Goshen.

She stopped by a well. Moses hid in the shadows.

"Please, can I have some water?" Moses heard her ask a young woman. "I have a long journey ahead of me."

Moses didn't know it, but the young woman was Miriam, his birth-sister. The young man with her was Aaron, his brother.

Miriam gave Tzipporah water and wished her luck on her journey.

Moses watched as Tzipporah mounted her camel and started toward the desert. Then he stepped forward.

When Miriam saw Moses she was stunned. She dropped the jug of water she was holding.

"Oh! I'm sorry. I'm so sorry," she stammered as she picked up the pieces of the broken jug.

"Please forgive me," she went on. "I did not expect to see you here, of all places, at our door. At last."

Moses laughed, confused. "Here at last?" he asked.

Miriam turned to Aaron and said, "Didn't I tell you? I knew he would return to us when he was ready."

"Shh!" Aaron warned his sister. "Do you want us flogged?"

Miriam ignored him. "I knew you cared about our freedom," she said to Moses.

Moses was bewildered. "Your freedom? Why should I care about that?" he asked.

"Because you're our brother," Miriam told him.

"What?" Moses asked. What was this woman saying? He was not her brother, he was Rameses' brother. He was a prince of Egypt!

"You mean, they never told you?" Miriam asked, seeing the confusion on his face. She reached out to him.

Moses pulled away. "Be careful, slave!" he warned.

At that moment, Aaron stepped forward to protect

his sister. "Please," he begged Moses. "Please forgive her. She's confused. She's tired. It's so hot, and she works so hard."

He grabbed Miriam by the waist and began to carry her away.

"You were born of our mother, Yocheved, and our father, Amram," Miriam called to Moses. "Our mother put you in a basket and set it afloat in the river. She did it to save your life. And with God's help you were spared. God saved you to be our deliverer."

My father is Pharaoh, he thought. *My mother is the Queen.*

But Miriam was not finished. "You are, Moses," she said. "You are the deliverer."

"Enough of this!" Moses shouted. He stepped toward Aaron and Miriam.

As he did, Miriam began to sing.
Hush now, my baby,
Be still, love, don't cry.
Sleep as you're rocked by the stream.
Sleep and remember
My last lullaby
So I'll be with you when you dream. . . .
Moses stopped. The song sounded familiar to him. Where had he heard it before?

Moses turned. He was confused and upset. The lullaby stirred his memory. Could what she had said be true?

No! Moses thought. He was not her brother, he was
Rameses' brother. His home was the palace, not here
among slaves.

He began to run. He had to get back home to the
palace.

Moses ran through streets and alleys. He pushed past
slaves and beggars, donkeys and goats. Finally, he
reached the palace grounds.

CHAPTER SIX
A NIGHTMARE

Moses entered the palace and looked up at the tall pillars. He was glad to be home.

Moses made his way back to his own room. Exhausted, he sat down against a stone column and quickly fell asleep. It was a restless sleep disturbed by a frightening nightmare.

In his sleep, Moses saw Pharaoh point a threatening finger. Guards attacked. He saw the guards push down women. They grabbed their babies and threw them into the river, to the crocodiles.

In his nightmare, Moses watched one mother—*his* mother—hide from the guards. He saw her put a baby in a basket. Lovingly, she placed it in the river and watched it float away.

Suddenly, Moses felt himself falling. He was tumbling into the river, toward the open mouths of the waiting crocodiles below.

He awoke with a start.

Could it be true? Was he really a Hebrew? Had

Pharaoh killed those babies? Moses was determined to find out.

He grabbed a torch and ran through the palace. He raced through the halls until he came to a vast, dark chamber. Its walls were covered with hieroglyphs, showing the history of Egypt.

Moses looked at the markings on the walls. An image caught his eye. It was a painting of Seti, sitting on his throne. He was pointing at a Hebrew baby boy, ordering that it be killed.

Moses fell to his knees. It was the same image he had seen in his dream.

So it was true, he realized. *It was all true.*

Moses imagined being thrown into the water. He imagined his own baby being torn away from him. He imagined the horrors of slavery.

Suddenly, he felt something. Someone had placed a hand on his head. Moses looked up and saw that it was Seti.

"Father," he pleaded. "Tell me you didn't do this."

"The Hebrews grew too numerous," Pharaoh explained. "They could have rebelled, taken my empire."

Tears filled Moses' eyes.

"Sometimes," Seti explained, "sacrifices must be made."

"But these were people, babies!" Moses cried out.

"Oh my son," Seti said. He reached out to embrace

Moses. But Moses did not want to be comforted. He broke away from Pharaoh and ran from the room.

He went to the Queen's watergarden. He sat there, staring at the water, and thought about the Hebrew people. He thought about his father, the man who had enslaved them.

He thought about his mother, the Queen. And about Rameses, his brother and best friend. He could not believe that they were not really his family.

Moses was still staring at the water when the Queen came to him.

"Is this where you found me?" he asked.

"Moses," she said. "Please try to understand."

"Understand what?" he asked. "That everything I am is a lie?"

"No," the Queen replied. "Understand that you are our son, and we love you."

"Why did you choose me?" Moses asked.

The Queen held Moses close. "We didn't choose you," she said. "The gods did."

CHAPTER SEVEN

RAMESES' PLANS

Several days later, Moses and Rameses were in the temple that they had damaged during their chariot race. Rebuilding the temple was to be Rameses' first project as Prince Regent.

Moses and Rameses stood on a platform and surveyed the ruins.

"With this project, I will prove my worth," Rameses told Moses. "I will restore this temple. I will make it more grand, more splendid than any other in Egypt."

Rameses placed his plans for the project on a table and showed them to Moses.

Moses looked at the plans. Then he looked around at the broken stone columns and statues. He saw slaves, some of them children, being forced to carry heavy stones and buckets of sand and water. Moses suddenly realized that these were *his* people.

"Centuries from now," Rameses boasted, "people will look at this temple and say, 'It was the great Rameses who built this.'"

But Moses wasn't listening. He was watching the slaves. On a scaffold, he saw an old man bent beneath a heavy load.

The man stumbled and fell.

Moses heard a guard shout "Get up!" at the old man.

The man struggled.

"Get up!" the guard shouted again. He whipped the man.

The old man slowly got to his feet. His knees and back were bent beneath his burden.

"Now move! Faster!" the guard commanded. He whipped the old man again and again.

Moses could not watch any longer.

"Stop it! Stop it!" Moses shouted. "Leave him alone!"

Rameses stopped talking. He looked at his brother, astonished at his strange reaction to a slave's cries.

Moses ran toward the scaffolding. When he reached the guard, he jumped on him and pushed him away from the old man. His push sent the guard back, off the high platform. He landed on the stone floor of the temple.

Everyone stopped to look at the fallen Egyptian. The guard was dead. Moses had killed him.

"There he is! He did it!" someone yelled, pointing at Moses.

"Get him! Get him!" a guard shouted.

Moses turned. He knew he had to escape. As he ran, a woman grabbed his arm.

"Moses!" she said.

He looked at her. It was Miriam, the woman he had met in Goshen. The woman who had called him "brother."

But Moses didn't dare stop. He pulled his arm away from Miriam and ran on.

He was near the gates of the palace when he heard the sounds of a horse and chariot chasing him.

"Moses! Moses!" the driver called.

Moses recognized the voice. It was Rameses.

Rameses jumped off his chariot and embraced his brother.

"You don't have to run," he told Moses. "I'll take care of everything."

"But I killed a man," Moses reminded him.

"I am Egypt," Rameses said proudly. "I am the morning and the evening star. I will make it so it never happened."

Even though Rameses could pardon him, Moses knew that his brother could never change the truth. Moses really was a Hebrew.

"You don't understand," said Moses. "All I have ever known to be true is a lie. I am not who you think I am."

"What are you talking about?" Rameses asked, confused.

"Ask the man I once called father," he said.

Moses began to walk away. Then he stopped, turned to Rameses, and said softly, "Good-bye, brother."

Then he ran off.

Moses ran from his past as a prince of Egypt. He became a wanderer, with no home or family.

CHAPTER EIGHT
A NEW LIFE

Moses walked for days, a lonely figure in the hot desert sand. Then he stepped on a sharp stone and his sandal tore.

Frustrated, he took off his sandals and threw them down. He ripped off his royal necklace and armbands and threw them into the sand, too.

Then Moses took off his ring, the one Rameses had given him. Moses looked at it for a long moment. But he couldn't bear to throw it away. He put it back on his finger, as a reminder of the brother he loved.

Suddenly, a fierce wind came and buried Moses in a deep sea of sand. Only the top of his head was visible.

Some time later, a camel came by. It noticed Moses' hair sticking out of the sand. It nibbled at it, then yanked Moses half out of the sand.

Moses looked up and saw the camel. With his last bit of strength, he reached for a water bag hanging from the camel's side. He grabbed hold of the bag and let the camel drag him through the sand.

After a while, they came to a water trough at the edge of a small village. Moses plunged his face into the trough and drank from it in huge gulps.

He was still drinking when he heard a young voice cry out, "Help! Stop!"

Moses looked up and saw three young girls. Some shepherds were chasing their animals from a well.

"Let our sheep drink," one of the girls cried.

"Get away," a shepherd told them.

While the girls argued with the men, Moses walked quietly over to where they had tied their camels. He untied the ropes. One by one, he chased the camels off.

"Hey," Moses called. "Were those yours?"

The men turned and saw their animals running away. "Wait!" they cried, and ran after them.

The girls hurried to Moses. "Thank you," they said. Suddenly, he lost his balance and fell back into the water.

"Don't worry, we'll help you," the oldest girl called down. She dropped a rope into the well. "Grab onto this," she said to Moses.

Moses grabbed the rope and listened as the girls struggled to pull him up. He heard another voice as their older sister joined them.

"What's going on?" she asked. Her sisters explained about the man in the well, and she helped to pull him out.

Moses was surprised when he saw who had saved

him. It was Tzipporah, the Midianite woman from the banquet!

Tzipporah was surprised as well.

"You!" she cried. She let go of the rope and Moses fell back into the water. Then she pulled him out again, and led him toward a large tent.

When they got to the tent, a large man came to the doorway. "Come in, come in," he said. "You are most welcome."

"This is my father, Jethro," Tzipporah told Moses. "The High Priest of Midian."

Jethro embraced Moses and said, "Tonight you shall be my honored guest."

That night there was a huge feast. Jethro bowed his head and said, "Let us give thanks for this bountiful food." Then he turned to Moses and said, "And let us give thanks to this brave young man whom we honor here tonight."

Moses thought about how his whole life had been a lie. He thought about the slaves in Egypt, and how they suffered because of his family.

"Please, sir," Moses said, "I wish you wouldn't. I have done nothing in my life worth honoring."

Jethro looked at Moses. "First you rescued Tzipporah from Egypt," he said. "Then you defended my younger daughters from the men at the well. You think that is nothing? It seems you don't know what is worthy of honor."

Moses realized that Tzipporah must have heard him when he distracted the guards at the palace. He sat in the warm glow of the fire and smiled as Jethro's guests ate, sang, and danced.

While the others celebrated, Moses thought of all the celebrations he had shared with Rameses. This one was not nearly as elegant as the ones in the palace, but it was certainly as joyous.

Moses stayed with Jethro and his family. Years passed, and Moses and Tzipporah fell in love and married.

CHAPTER NINE
A DESERT MIRACLE

One day, while Moses was tending sheep near the mountain of Horeb, a lamb ran off. Moses chased after it, and found himself in a quiet rock formation.

Before him stood a burning bush.

The branches and leaves of the bush blazed, but they were not harmed by the flames. Moses put his staff into the flames, but the wood did not burn. He stretched his hand toward it, but he was not hurt.

Moses stood awestruck. Suddenly, he heard a voice. "Moses! Moses!" the voice called.

Moses turned, but saw no one.

"Moses! Moses!" the voice called to him again. "Take off your sandals. You are standing in a holy place."

Moses took off his sandals. "Who are you?" he asked.

"I am that I am," the voice said.

"What?" Moses asked. "I don't understand."

"I am the God of your fathers, of Abraham, Isaac, and Jacob."

And of Amram, Yocheved, Miriam, and Aaron, Moses

thought. *And my God, too.*

"I have seen the oppression of My people in Egypt," God continued. "I have heard their cries. I shall take them out of slavery and bring them to their promised land. And so unto Pharaoh I shall send you."

Moses stared at the flames, too stunned to react.

"You shall lead my people to freedom," God told Moses.

"Me?" Moses asked. "Who am I to lead these people? They'll never believe me. They won't even listen."

"I shall teach you what to say."

"But I was their enemy," Moses protested. "I was the Prince of Egypt, the son of the man who killed their children. You've chosen the wrong messenger."

"Who made man's mouth?" God asked angrily. "Did not I? Now go!"

Moses stepped back, too afraid to look at the burning bush.

Then God spoke softly. "I shall be with you when you speak to the people," He assured Moses. "I shall be with you, too, when you speak to Pharaoh."

Moses felt his confidence growing.

"Take your staff in your hands," God told him. "With it you shall do My wonders. With it, you shall lead the Hebrew people to freedom."

The voice faded away and the flames subsided, leaving the bush unharmed.

Moses looked at the bush for a moment. Then he took his staff and led his sheep home. He told Tzipporah what he had seen. He told her that God had spoken to him, and that he would lead God's people to freedom.

"But Moses," Tzipporah protested, "you are just one man."

Moses pointed to Tzipporah's family. They were outside doing their daily chores.

"Look at your family," he told her. "They're free. They have hopes and dreams. That is what I want for my people," he told her. "That is why I *must* do the task that God has given me."

Moses thought of his father, who had ordered the

death of the Hebrew babies. He thought of his brother, Rameses, who ordered the slaves to erect great temples. Moses knew that somehow he had to put a stop to it.

Tzipporah looked lovingly at her husband. She embraced him and said softly, "I'm coming with you."

CHAPTER TEN
BITTERSWEET REUNION

Moses and Tzipporah began their journey back to Egypt.

As they traveled, Moses wondered how he would feel confronting Seti, the man he once called father. He also thought about seeing Rameses again after so many years. As Moses and Tzipporah passed through the palace gates, Moses asked to see Pharaoh. They were led into the palace banquet hall. Pharaoh was sitting on his throne, conferring with his advisors.

Then Pharaoh looked up.

Moses was shocked. It was Rameses!

Rameses hurried off the throne. "Moses! Is it really you? Where have you been?" Rameses asked.

Before Moses could answer, Rameses lifted him off the ground and held him in a warm embrace.

Moses was caught up in the excitement of seeing Rameses again. For a moment, he forgot why he had returned to Egypt.

When Rameses put him down, Moses stepped back

and eyed his brother. "Look at you! You're Pharaoh," he said.

They hugged again, and Moses added, "It's so good to see you."

Then the palace priests, Hotep and Huy, stepped forward. They reminded Rameses that Moses had killed an Egyptian guard.

Rameses wasn't interested in hearing about Moses' crime. He was just happy that his brother had returned.

But the mention of the guard reminded Moses why he had come back. His face grew serious.

"Rameses," Moses said. "Things cannot be as they were."

"I don't see why not," Rameses answered, smiling.

But Moses did not smile back. He told Rameses that God had spoken to him.

"God commands that you let the Hebrew people go," Moses told him.

"Commands?" Rameses asked, shocked that anyone would command the Pharaoh.

He almost expected Moses to laugh. When they were boys, Moses was always playing jokes on Rameses. But now, Moses remained serious.

Rameses led Moses to a balcony. "Look," he said, pointing to the beautiful temples, palaces, and gardens. "A far greater Egypt than that of my father," he told Moses.

Moses looked out over the same balcony. He told Rameses that he did not see temples and palaces. All he could see were slaves. There were thousands of them, being beaten and struggling beneath heavy loads.

"I cannot change what you see," Rameses told Moses. "Nor will I let your people go."

Moses looked at his brother sadly. He took off the ring that Rameses had given him long ago. He placed it on the arm of the throne.

"I'm sorry," he said.

Then Moses tried to warn him of the danger of defying God's will.

But Rameses would not listen. He picked up the ring, held it in his hand, and stared at it. Then he declared, "I do not know this God, nor will I let your people go. I will not be the weak link."

Rameses glared at Moses. Then he said, "Tell your people that as of this day, their workload has been doubled. And they have you to thank for it."

As Moses and Tzipporah left the palace, Moses realized that he had spoken the truth. Things could not be as they were. His warm, loving relationship with Rameses had ended.

He had a new family now. A new people, and a mission to gain them their freedom.

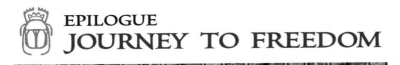

EPILOGUE
JOURNEY TO FREEDOM

Moses knew that he could not let his people down.

Again and again, he returned to meet with Rameses.

Each time, Moses asked him to let the Hebrew people go. He warned Rameses that if he didn't, a terrible plague would follow.

But Rameses refused again and again.

Each time, God brought forth a new plague.

There were ten plagues in all.

Frogs swarmed through the palace. Locusts devastated the fields. Flies swarmed, cattle died, and darkness fell.

With each plague, the Egyptian people suffered more and more.

When the tenth plague struck, every firstborn Egyptian male, including Rameses' own son, died.

Moses returned to the palace and found Rameses bent in grief.

Rameses would not look at Moses. He gently pulled a cloth over his dead son's head and said coldly, "You and your people have my permission to go."

Without a word, Moses left the palace.

As soon as he was outside, he was overcome with sadness. He fell down and cried for his brother. Then he went into Goshen and gave his people the news.

The Hebrews left Egypt that very night. They marched across the desert toward the Red Sea.

But Rameses changed his mind. He refused to give up his slaves. He refused to let Moses beat him.

Gathering his powerful army, Rameses set out across the desert to recapture the Hebrews.

When the Hebrews reached the Red Sea, they saw the vast expanse of water in front of them. Behind them, they saw the Egyptian army rapidly approaching.

The Hebrews were trapped! Terrified, they turned to Moses for guidance.

Feeling God's power, Moses walked to the edge of the sea. He looked at the staff he held in his hand.

"With this staff," God had said, "you shall do My wonders."

Moses put his staff into the sea, and the waters miraculously parted. The Hebrew people walked between the walls of water, toward the far shore.
The Egyptians began to follow.

But as soon as the Hebrews had reached safety, the waters flooded the passageway.

Only Rameses survived. He stood on the Egyptian shore and looked out over the water in despair.